# Gilbert
## The Great Fish

Psalms 139:14

Written by Jason Cooper

Illustrated by Lisa Bohart

*AuthorHouse™*
*1663 Liberty Drive*
*Bloomington, IN 47403*
*www.authorhouse.com*
*Phone: 1-800-839-8640*

*First published by AuthorHouse  10/20/2011*

*ISBN:      978-1-4670-4289-5 (sc)*

*Library of Congress Control Number: 2011918108*
*Printed in the United States of America*

authorHOUSE®

*To my nieces and nephews*

*Jeremiah, Dennai, Gracey,*
*Aubrey, Ty, & Sarah*

*who are always able*
*to make Uncle Jason smile*

From the time he was just a minnow, Gilbert's mother always told him that God had a plan for his life. She would say, "You are a special fish, Gilbert," and "God is going to use you for something really big one day".

This would always make him feel special. And he was special. Not just because of what Mother Fish would tell him, but Gilbert was different from all the other fish in a lot of ways.

For starters, Gilbert was *GIGANTIC*!  Even as just a fingerling, he was twice the size of every other fish in his *entire* school! He would have to sit in the back of his class just so the other fish could see the teacher. Sometimes, his classmates would make fun of him because of how big he was.

3

When he got home from school, he would cry as he told his mother what the mean fish had said.

Mother Fish would comfort him by gently holding his fin and praying that God would show Gilbert just how special he was.

"Mom, does God really think I'm special?" Gilbert asked.

Mother Fish would smile and say, "Of course he does, you silly fish. If God didn't have something special planned for your life, He wouldn't have made you in the first place!"

This would make Gilbert feel a lot better and he would completely forget about what the other fish had said to him earlier that day.

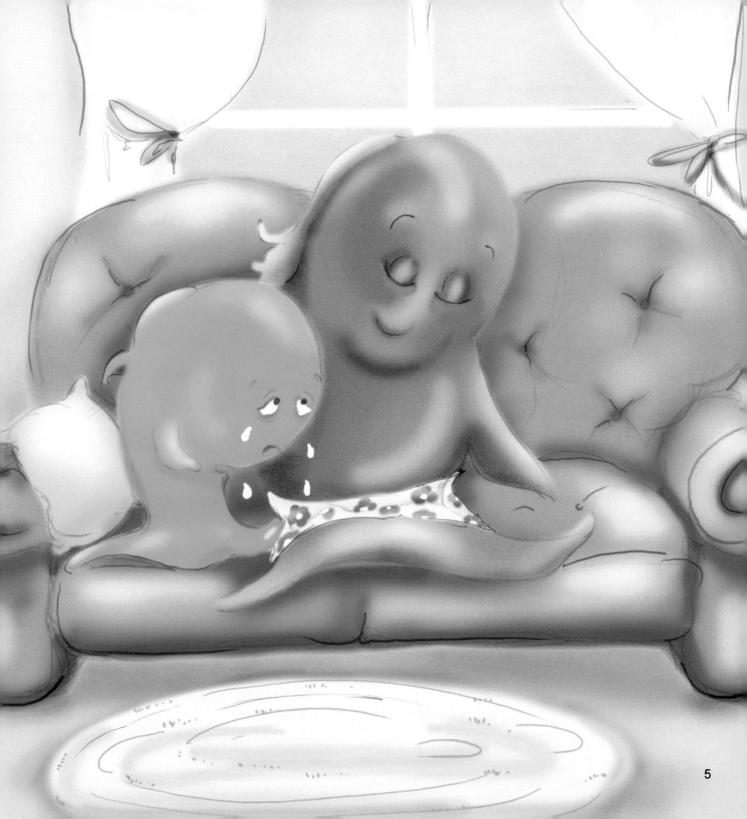

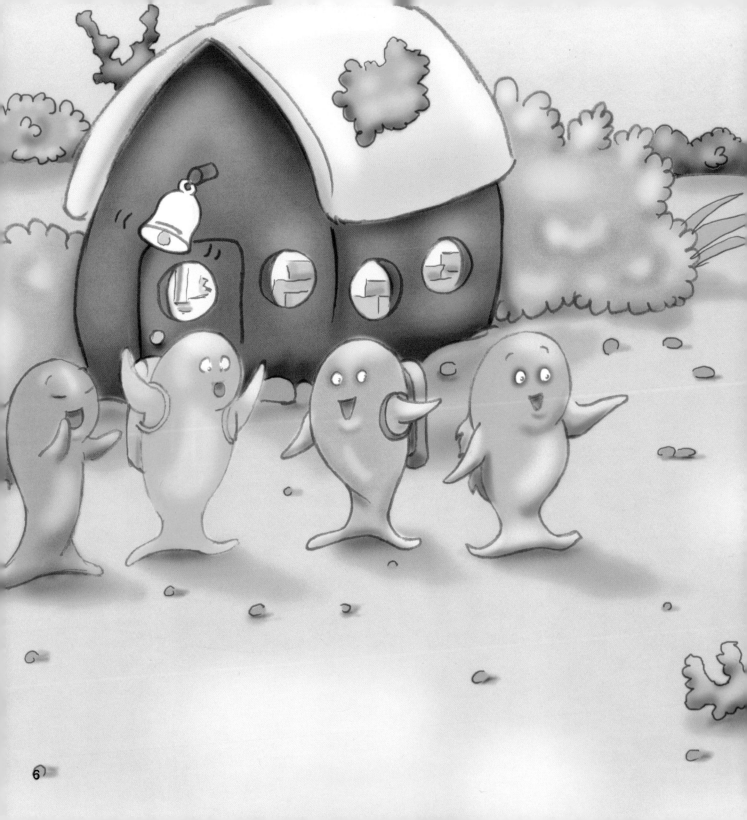

As time went on, Gilbert continued to grow bigger and bigger. The mean fish at school continued to make fun of him, and as hard as he tried to ignore what they would say, it still hurt his feelings.

"Mom," he would ask through his tears, "Why do I have to be so big? Why can't I be the same size as all the other fish in my school? Then maybe they wouldn't make fun of me!"

Mother Fish would gently hold his fin just like all the other times and try to encourage Gilbert to trust in God because she knew He had a plan for his life.

As he grew older and bigger still, he could barely fit into his house. His mother would encourage Gilbert to talk to God whenever the other fish would say mean things.

She would say, "God has something special for you, Gilbert. Why don't you ask Him to show you what it is? If you ask, He will answer you."

Gilbert would *squeeeeze* through the door to his room and pray, "God, I don't understand why I am so different than all the other fish. Mom says you made me this way on purpose and you have something special for me to do one day. Is that true?"

God would answer, "Yes, Gilbert. I made you just how I wanted you. If you will just trust me and be patient, one day you will understand."

Day after day, he would ask God these same questions, and God would give him the same answers. Sometimes it would help. But sometimes it wouldn't.

Time went by and, before long, Gilbert had grown into one of the biggest fish in the *entire* ocean. The other fish who used to make fun of him were now scared of him because he was *SO* big. He couldn't even fit into his own house anymore! They had to build a *GINORMOUS* room just for him to sleep in!

Gilbert tried and tried to keep believing that God had a reason for making him so big. He prayed and prayed just like his mother had taught him to.

"God, I don't understand why I am so big" Gilbert prayed again. "You always told me that you had a reason for making me this big. But when will you show me what it is? Nobody likes me. I don't even fit in my own house!"

Poor Gilbert just couldn't take it anymore. He decided he was going to swim away from home.

But just as he was about to leave, God spoke to him and said "I have made you just how I wanted you. And I have a something special for you to do."

"What can I do when I am so big?" Gilbert asked. "I won't be able to do anything like I am!"

But God answered and said, "Just trust me, Gilbert. When the time comes, I will tell you what I need you to do. You will understand soon."

So Gilbert decided not to swim away like he wanted to. Instead, he decided to listen and wait for God to tell him what to do.

One day, a *HUGE* storm came. All of the fish could see that there were big waves on the surface. It made it hard to see because the water was becoming murky with mud stirred up by the storm.

As the storm raged on above, God spoke to Gilbert and said, "It's time. I have something for you to do."

Gilbert heard God's voice and asked, "What is it, God?"

"Swim up towards the surface, and I will show you when you get there," God answered.

So Gilbert swam toward the surface where he could see the waves were really big. "Ok, God. I'm here…now what?" Gilbert asked.

But there was no answer from God.

All of a sudden, Gilbert heard a big *SPLASH* not too far ahead of him! He swam closer to see what it was. As he was swimming, Gilbert noticed the waves and storm had stopped and the water was completely still...Everything was quiet. The water was still a bit cloudy, but as Gilbert got closer to where he heard the splash come from, he began to see something in the water. It was a *MAN*!

Gilbert didn't know what to do. He had never seen a man before – only the boats they would ride in.

He watched as the boat the man had fallen out of moved further and further away. The man was sinking fast! Gilbert knew he had to do something. He had to help! But how? What could he do? It was a three-day swim to land and the nearest boat had just sailed away, leaving the man to drown.

At last, Gilbert decided that he would take the man to land himself.

"God," he prayed, "Help the man not to drown, and I will take him back to land."

As he prayed, Gilbert swam as fast as he could down to the man and snatched him up in his mouth. He was so big that he was able to swallow the man whole! Then, Gilbert set off.

He swam as fast as he could and didn't stop. While he was swimming, he began to hear a noise coming from inside his belly. It was the man! He was praying!!! He was talking to God just like Gilbert does!

Knowing that the man was asking God for help made Gilbert want to swim even faster.

After swimming and swimming, Gilbert finally began to see land. But now what? Should he spit him out and let him swim the rest of the way?

"What should I do, God?" Gilbert asked out loud.

God spoke to him and said, "Take the man up to dry land and spit him out there."

So Gilbert did exactly what God told him to do. He spit the man out onto the land and turned back toward the deeper water.

Gilbert stayed in the shallower water to catch his breath and watched to see if the man was ok.

As he was watching, the man got on his knees, and Gilbert could hear him praying, "Okay, God, I will go to Nineveh and do what you told me to do." After that, the man got up and walked away.

During his swim home, Gilbert felt proud that he was able to help the man. He couldn't wait to get back to tell his mother and everyone else what had happened.

It felt as if God was saying, "I'm proud of you, Gilbert. You did exactly what I made you to do."

From that day forward, one thing was for sure – Gilbert never doubted God's plan for his life again.

CPSIA information can be obtained
at www.ICGtesting.com
Printed in the USA
LVIC041140240112
265347LV00004B